WELCOME TO

Beast Quest

Collect the special coins in this book.
You will earn one gold coin for
every chapter you read.

Once you have finished all the chapters,
find out what to do with your gold coins at
the back of the book.

With special thanks to Cherith Baldry

To Charlie, Sam and Thomas

www.beastquest.co.uk

ORCHARD BOOKS

First published in Great Britain in 2010 by The Watts Publishing Group
This edition published in 2015 by The Watts Publishing Group

11 13 15 17 19 20 18 16 14 12

Text © 2010 Beast Quest Limited.
Cover and interior illustrations by Steve Sims
© Beast Quest Limited 2010

Beast Quest is a registered trademark of Beast Quest Limited
Series created by Beast Quest Limited, London

A CIP catalogue record for this book is available from the British Library.

ISBN 978 1 40830 725 0

Printed and bound by CPI Group (UK) Ltd, Croydon, CR0 4YY

The paper and board used in this book are made from wood from responsible sources

Orchard Books
An imprint of Hachette Children's Group
Part of The Watts Publishing Group Limited
Carmelite House, 50 Victoria Embankment, London EC4Y 0DZ

An Hachette UK Company
www.hachette.co.uk
www.hachettechildrens.co.uk

FanG
THE BAT FIEND

BY ADAM BLADE

ORCHARD

KAYONIA

THE GOLDEN VALLEY

MEATON

CONTENTS

HAIL, YOUNG WARRIORS!

Tom has set out on a Quest of his own choosing, and I have the honour of helping with magic learnt from the greatest teacher of them all: my master, Aduro. Tom's challenges will be great: a new kingdom, a lost mother and six more Beasts under Velmal's spell.

Tom isn't just fighting to save a kingdom. He's fighting to save those lives closest to him and to prove that love can conquer evil. Can it?

Tom will only find out by staying strong and keeping the flame of hope alive.

As long as no foul wind blows it out…

Yours truly,

The apprentice, Marc

PROLOGUE

Toby grasped his pickaxe, wincing
at the pain from his blistered hands.
He could hardly see the wall in front
of him. Frustration at his dim sight
swept over him and he attacked the
rock face even harder than usual. The
blows echoed off the wall, blending
with the strokes of the other workers
beside him, and the clink of the
chains that bound them.

*More gold…*Toby thought wearily. *More riches flowing like a river through the Golden Valley of Kayonia.*

Pausing to ease his aching shoulders, he listened to the grunts and groans of his fellow slaves.

They're all content to be blind, as long as their town has wealth. Toby gripped his axe harder, as if he wanted to break the handle. *But I'm not content…*

"Hey, what do you think you're doing?"

Toby jumped at the whispering voice of Jed, the man working next to him.

"Get back to work, or the master will punish you," Jed said.

Toby's anger wrestled with his fear.
"I don't care!" he declared, standing
up straight. "I'm sick of being a slave.
I'm going to break free of this place!
Who's with me?"

There was no reply, except for the
renewed hammering of pickaxes.
Toby could feel the other slaves'
fear; they were acting like he wasn't

there. He understood why they were scared. Their master seemed to move about them in total silence, until he announced himself with echoing shrieks and screeches that made Toby's ears hurt.

"Don't be a fool," Jed said in a low voice. Toby could hardly see him swing his pickaxe, because of his poor eyesight. "You can't escape. The master's not like us. He can see in the dark, for one thing. He could be watching us right now." Both miners looked around fearfully.

Toby shivered. He remembered how, when they first came to work in the mine, the master would snatch up anyone who disobeyed him and carry them off. Many workers had been taken that way – and not a single one had ever returned.

Toby's limbs ached, and stinging sweat trickled into his eyes. *I can't stand any more of this. I've got to take the risk...*

He weighed the pickaxe in his hand. "Maybe this will break my chains," he murmured. "And maybe I can run fast enough to escape the master's clutches. Maybe—"

He broke off as he felt Jed's hand grip his shoulder.

"This is lunacy," Jed muttered. "Get back to work, before the master sees you."

Toby shook Jed's hand off. "You stay if you want. I'd rather die trying to escape than keep slaving away here."

He began to hack at his chains.
Tiny sparks lit up the darkness as the
blows fell. Toby could feel the chain
start to break.

Soon I'll be free!

The whispered voices of the other
slaves came at him from all sides.

"Stop!"

"You'll get us all in trouble!"

Toby ignored their protests. The
chains fell from his legs. He moved
away from the rock face, half
crouching, his hands scraping the
floor. Somewhere along the tunnel,
on the way to the cavern where they
all slept, was a mine shaft leading
to the surface. The noise of the other
miners died away behind him; all he
could hear now was the sound of his

own panting breath as he scrambled for freedom.

He peered along the tunnel, blinking in an attempt to clear his vision. He realised he could see walls lit by a pale grey light.

My sight's already improving, Toby thought. *I won't be blind forever!*

The mine shaft was just ahead. The light grew stronger, until he stood at the bottom of the shaft where he could see a patch of blue sky high above.

Scrabbling for ledges and cracks, Toby began to climb. At first it was hard to find footholds, but he soon worked himself into a rhythm. The blue circle of sky grew closer and closer.

Nearly there...

Then Toby heard a fierce shriek coming from below him in the mine shaft. He froze in terror.

"The master..." he croaked.

Peering down into the weak light, Toby spotted vast leathery wings and two eyes that glowed orange as the giant bat flew up towards him. It opened its mouth, revealing blade-sharp teeth – and before Toby could dodge, they closed over his

shoulder. With a cry of pain, Toby
lost his grip and slid down the shaft,
hitting the ground with a *thud*.

Toby caught sight of those terrible
teeth glinting above him. Unable to
look away, he wished his eyesight
had never improved.

He didn't want to see what the
master was going to do to him.

THE ROAD TO THE NORTH

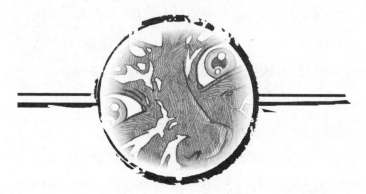

Tom wiped his streaming eyes. "The sooner we're out of these stinking cornfields, the better," he said.

Elenna nodded. "I can't wait."

Tom gagged as he tried not to breathe too deeply. In vanquishing Muro the Rat Monster, he had destroyed the windmill that created the awful smell filling the air. The stench was fading away – but not as fast as Tom would have liked.

Silver the wolf scampered about in narrow circles, while Tom's stallion, Storm, gave his bridle an impatient shake; their animal friends were just as eager to get away from the cornfields as they were.

"We have four more Quests to complete here in Kayonia," Tom went on. "Let's get them over with quickly."

"Right," said Elenna. "Only then can we go back to Avantia."

Tom sighed. "It would be great to go home now," he said. "But we can't leave yet. Let's see where we have to go next."

Pulling out the Amulet of Avantia, which he kept on a thong around his neck, Tom watched as the path to their next Quest was magically traced across its surface. "It's telling us to go north, into the mountains," he told Elenna.

His friend peered more closely at the amulet as some tiny letters appeared. "The Golden Valley," she read aloud.

Just beside the words, Tom saw a picture of a curious red jewel. "That must be the next ingredient we have to find," he said.

Tom had only just discovered that Freya, Mistress of the Beasts, was his mother. Now she was under the spell of evil Velmal. Tom had to find six ingredients to make a potion that would free her, but the ingredients were scattered across the realm of Kayonia, each one guarded by an Evil Beast.

"At least the Golden Valley looks like it won't smell as bad as this place," Elenna said, waving a hand in front of her nose, a look of disgust on her face.

Tom examined the map more closely. "You're right. There are lakes, reservoirs and rivers running in all directions," he said.

He let the amulet fall against his chest as he climbed into the saddle.

"Let's get moving," he said, reaching down to help Elenna up behind him. With Silver already scampering ahead, Tom urged Storm into a canter.

To his relief, the smell faded even
more as they left the cornfields
behind. A breeze started to blow and
the air became cool and fresh.

But the sun was sinking quickly,
and soon it set in a blaze of scarlet

and gold. The twilight deepened and stars appeared in the sky. The three moons rose, but they weren't bright enough to light the way.

"It's too dark to go on," Tom said, feeling a stab of frustration. Here in Kayonia, the sun seemed to rise and set as it pleased.

"Storm and Silver are slowing down," Elenna pointed out. "They think it's time to sleep!"

Tom saw she was right. Storm was plodding along with his head low, and Silver, who usually bounded ahead, padded quietly beside the horse.

"We'd better make camp," he said. "The trouble is, we don't know how long the night will last. It could be over in a moment, or be as long as two Avantian nights."

"How are we supposed to plan a Quest in a world like this?" Elenna asked.

"We'll find a way," said Tom, slipping out of the saddle. "We always do."

Tom stared into darkness. A face floated in front of him. *Freya...*

The features were familiar, and yet strange. He should have felt comforted by the sight of his mother, but he was horrified. When Tom had last seen her, she had been strong and beautiful, though fierce. Now his mother's face was disfigured by

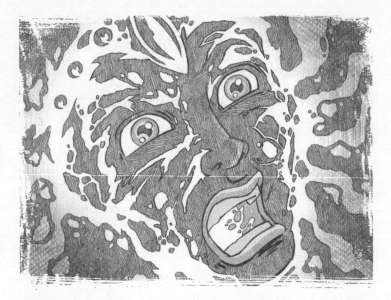

cracks, the edges of which sizzled, as if she were being burned from inside. As Tom gazed at her, she let out a cry of pain.

Mother, hold on! I'll bring the potion to save you!

Tom reached out to her, but Freya's face disappeared like fading mist.

Tom suddenly became aware of the

cold, grassy ground beneath him, and
the blanket around his legs. Beside
him, Elenna slept soundly, wrapped
in her own blanket. Beyond them,
Storm and Silver dozed contentedly.

It had been a dream – a dream sent
by Velmal to taunt him.

Rage burned in Tom's heart.
Throwing his blanket aside, he
rose to his feet and drew his sword.
Holding the blade up, he faced the
hills where the first pale light of
dawn was appearing on the horizon.

"Beware, Velmal!" he hissed. "While
there's blood in my veins, I'll rescue
my mother from your evil magic!"

2

THE GOLDEN VALLEY

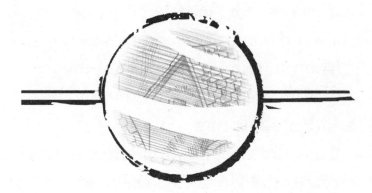

"Elenna, we have to hurry," said Tom, shaking his friend awake and setting about saddling Storm. "Freya's time is running out."

Elenna got up quickly to help and they were on the move before the sun had risen high. It was a huge effort for Tom to stay upright and grip the reins. His limbs ached with weariness; his dream seemed to have sapped all his energy.

He could tell that Elenna was also exhausted. She leant against him in the saddle, hardly saying a word.

The sun climbed rapidly in the sky. Tom knew this was going to be another short day.

They drew to a halt where a narrow stream trickled across the road.

"We'd better rest and have something to eat," he said.

Elenna slid to the ground without replying and knelt beside the stream to splash her face and hands. Tom led Storm to the water's edge and Silver padded along beside him.

When the wolf had taken a drink, he trotted up to Storm, his plumy tail waving, and nudged him playfully on his foreleg. Storm snorted angrily and swiped a hoof at Silver. The wolf quickly sprang back, out of range.

"Storm, stop that!" Elenna snapped.

"Tell Silver to stop bothering him, then," Tom said irritably.

Elenna started to reply, then clapped her hand over her mouth.

Tom gazed at her in dismay. *What's happening? We* never *argue!* "I'm sorry, Elenna," he said quietly. "It's these Kayonian days. We're not getting enough sleep, and it's making us tetchy."

"You're right," Elenna responded. "I'm sorry, too."

Tom was glad that the quarrel

was over, but as he went to get food from his saddlebag, he couldn't stop feeling uneasy.

If we're like this after only two Quests in Kayonia, how much more damage will this place do to our friendship before the end?

Two more swift Kayonian days and nights passed before Tom and his friends reached the road that would take them to the Golden Valley. It ran alongside a river. Tom stared at the rushing water for a long time.

"The current shouldn't be as fast as this," he said. "And there's something else odd about the way it's flowing..."

"I know," said Elenna. "It's almost as if…" She broke off with a gasp of astonishment. "Tom, look at that!"

Ahead, Tom looked up at a massive waterfall thundering over a cliff. He gazed at it for a moment, puzzled, until he realised what he was seeing. Instead of cascading down the cliff, the river was pouring upwards from the ground!

"The water's flowing uphill… Impossible…" Tom murmured. The hairs on his neck prickled, as if someone was watching him. He glanced all around, but he couldn't see anything move. "Unless," he went on, "it's the work of dark magic."

"Or maybe it's just one more strange thing about Kayonia,"

Elenna suggested, staring in astonishment at the waterfall. "But we'd better keep our eyes peeled, whatever the case may be."

She called Silver to walk close beside them as Tom guided Storm right up to the pool at the base of the cliff. The waterfall was surrounded by thick bushes and jagged rocks. Only when they drew closer to it could Tom see a narrow path twisting back and forth up the steep slope.

"That looks dangerous," he said, dismounting. "I'll lead Storm. You stay down here and keep watch."

Tom held his shield in front of him as they climbed to the top of the waterfall. It was hard to keep his footing on the loose rocks; if anyone

attacked him, defending himself
would be tricky.

He heaved a sigh of relief when
he reached the top of the cliff and
saw the Golden Valley stretching in
front of him. The road they travelled
on continued beside the river, with
rolling moorland stretching away
on either side to the edges of the
valley.

But Tom's relief didn't last long.
There was something unexpected
about the landscape in front of him,
and for a moment he couldn't work
out what it was.

"You can come up now," he called,
beckoning to Elenna.

"What's the matter?" his friend
asked, as she and Silver joined him

at the top of the path. "You look worried."

"Something's wrong," Tom replied, pulling the amulet from his tunic. "Look," he went on, pointing to the road they were following. "This should lead us to a town. There are buildings and other roads quite clearly marked on the map. But there's nothing up ahead of us – just that lake."

"I've got a bad feeling about this," Elenna murmured, peering over Tom's shoulder at the map.

Tom tucked the amulet back into his tunic. "But the map hasn't ever steered us the wrong way before," he said.

Tom mounted Storm again and

helped Elenna up behind him. Together they headed down into the valley. As they drew closer to the lake, Tom spotted dark shapes poking up through the surface.

Realisation hit him, and he shivered.

He guided Storm to the lake's edge and jumped down from the saddle. Elenna sprang down after him; together they walked to the lapping water. There were shapes beneath the lake's surface.

"Elenna, look!" Tom said, pointing. "That slanting beam looks like the roof of a house, and those gnarled branches must be the tops of trees."

"I can see…stables," said Elenna, squinting. "There's a barn and a

market stall. Tom! It's a whole
sunken city!"

"How did that happen?" Tom
wondered aloud.

Side by side, Tom and Elenna
knelt down to peer more closely at
the underwater city. Silver sniffed
suspiciously at the water.

"Don't drink it," Elenna warned him, laying a hand on the ruff of fur around his neck.

Tom gazed closer at the structures beneath the water. "Look at that wall," he said, pointing to a huge edifice that surrounded the sunken buildings. The grey stones were flecked with gold. "Someone built that to keep the water in. This looks like a lake, but it's man-made, with water that must have been diverted from the river."

Elenna's eyes widened in surprise. "Why would anyone flood a city? And what happened to all the people living there?"

Tom was asking himself the same questions. Then he shook his head.

"There's no time to worry about this," he said decisively. "We have a Quest to complete."

Tom looked at the amulet again. Their path led further along the valley, into a rocky area in the far north, which skirted the edge of what looked like another lake.

Above the second lake, the shape of a bat slowly appeared.

"There's our next Beast!" Tom exclaimed.

Cold fingers seemed to crawl down his spine as he saw letters scrawling across the map, spelling out a dreaded name.

FANG.

THE BLIND MINER

In the saddle, Elenna took Storm's reins, while Tom drew his sword and held his shield ready as they headed along the gorge, skirting the edge of the lake. At the far end, the road rejoined the river. Tom and Elenna exchanged a glance of surprise as they saw that the riverbed was dry.

"I wonder what happened here," Elenna said.

"I don't know," Tom replied, warily looking about. "Maybe Velmal's magic is to blame?"

Suddenly Storm halted. "What...?" Elenna exclaimed, lurching in the saddle. "Why have we...?"

Her voice trailed off. Instead of the lake marked on the map, the ground dropped down into a vast, empty crater.

"This must have been the lake," Tom said. "But now it's bone dry."

There were dark holes cut in the side of the opposite slope of the crater, with tracks leading to the openings. "Those look like shafts," said Tom. "Someone must have drained this place and flooded the town."

"I still don't understand why," said Elenna.

"Maybe there are mines here," Tom suggested.

While he was speaking, he heard the clink of a hoof on stone and the creaking of cart wheels. Looking down into the pit, he spotted a horse-drawn wagon a short distance away, slowly trundling down a winding path that snaked across the crater. The driver was walking beside the horse with his hand on the bridle.

"He might be able to tell us something about this place," Tom said. "Let's catch him up."

Elenna guided Storm carefully down the slope, keeping to the side of the path and avoiding the deep dips and ruts where Storm could injure himself.

Silver padded a little way ahead, raising his muzzle from time to time to sniff the air. *Silver always knows when danger is near*, Tom thought. *And I'm sure there's danger here!*

As they approached, Tom could see that the wagon was loaded with hammers and pickaxes. "I was right," he whispered to Elenna. "They *are* mining round here."

As he spoke, the wagon driver halted and turned towards Tom and Elenna. He was a big man with a broad face as red as his hair. "Who goes there?" he called.

Tom was surprised the man had

heard their quiet approach, and
even more surprised at the alarm in
his voice.

"We're travellers," Tom replied,
as Elenna reined in Storm to stand
behind the wagon. Tom's gaze fell on
the pickaxes. "We're, um…looking

for the local mine," he said.

"Yes, is this it?" Elenna added, playing along.

A grin split the miner's face, revealing a mouthful of blackened teeth. "Ah, you must be the new workers," he said.

Tom noticed something strange about the man's face. He walked closer and saw that the miner's eyes had a grey film over them. *He's blind!*

"We've been short-handed since we, er…lost Toby," the man went on. "What good luck! They sent two of you!"

A chill ran through Tom. "What happened to Toby?" he asked.

The miner's smile disappeared.

"Never you mind," he said. "Follow me. I'll show you the way."

Elenna turned around in the saddle to look at Tom. "Why are you—" she began in a whisper.

Tom raised a finger to his lips. If the miner was blind, his hearing was probably strong enough to hear even a whisper...

He realised that Elenna must be confused about why they were going to the mine, when they should be tracking down a Beast. He pulled out the amulet and pointed to the picture. Elenna's eyes widened in understanding – the image of Fang had appeared above the empty lake.

The miner led his horse further down into the pit. Tom and Elenna followed on Storm, with Silver padding at the stallion's heels. Tom marvelled at the blind miner's skill: how he was able to guide the horse and wagon by following the ruts in the road.

"He can't see," Tom whispered, hoping that the rumble of the cart would cover his voice, "but he knows the path so well, he never trips."

Elenna nodded. "The horse knows where he's going, too."

The horse pulling the wagon was old and worn out; he looked as if he had spent years dragging the wagon up and down the path.

"Isn't it hard, working in the mine when you're blind?" Tom asked the man, gently.

The man shrugged. "It's dark in there anyway. I lost my sight from being down there for so long, and—" He broke off with a gasp and paused as if he was listening to something Tom could not hear. "But it's a price worth paying," he went on.

Tom and Elenna exchanged a surprised glance. Tom thought that the man sounded almost afraid. *Why doesn't he want anyone to hear him complaining? There is no one around to hear him, except us.*

They were drawing closer to the bottom of the pit. Then, at a turn in the path, the miner's horse slipped on a loose stone. He stumbled and would have fallen if not for the shafts of the wagon holding him up.

The miner let out a yell of dismay as he bent over the horse's hoof. He felt it carefully. "He's lame!"

Tom slid down from Storm's back and went to have a look. The horse couldn't put his foot on the ground, and was sweating and rolling its eyes in pain.

"He should be all right," Tom assured the miner. "He needs to have his leg bandaged, and rest for a while."

"But how am I supposed to make my delivery?" the miner asked, his face pale and sweaty. "The master will be so angry!"

"Surely your master will understand?" said Tom.

"Oh, no, no!" The miner was

wringing his hands and almost
sobbing. "He'll punish me if I don't
deliver the tools on time." He fell to
his knees in front of Tom. "You have
to help me!"

Tom glanced up at Elenna and saw
she shared his surprise. *This 'master'
must be really fearsome to frighten
his workers this much*, he thought.

INTO THE MINE

"Yes, of course we'll help you," Tom said. "You can borrow my horse to pull the cart to the mine."

Relief spread over the miner's face. "Th-thank you," he stammered. "I'll never forget this."

Fumbling with the harness, he untied his horse from the cart.

Elenna held the miner's horse by the bridle while Tom helped him harness Storm in its place.

"I'm sorry, boy," Tom said, rubbing the stallion's nose. "I know you're not a carthorse, but it won't be for long."

Storm tossed his mane and blew out a long snort.

This time Tom led the way down to the bottom of the pit, carefully steering Storm around the ruts in the path. The miner led his own limping horse, and Elenna brought up the rear with Silver.

While Tom was glad to help, a knot of fear was gathering in his stomach. *Surely no* man *could scare the miner so badly? But a* Beast *could*, he thought.

"Fang…" Tom murmured aloud.

When they reached the bottom of

the pit, the miner took them to the end of a metal railway track, which disappeared into one of the dark tunnels. Several battered wooden wagons sat on the tracks.

"That's a clever idea," Tom said.

"I've seen something like it in Avantia," Elenna said, following Silver, who had bounded up to sniff the cart with his nose.

"So have I," Tom replied. "But not often." He turned to the miner. "Is this how you get supplies into the mine?"

"That's right," the man replied. "Tools, supplies and workers. You'll be going that way, too."

A thrill of excitement passed through Tom. *I'm getting close to the Beast!*

"You can't go down the mine,"
Tom told Storm as he unharnessed
him from the cart and led him to
a twisted tree not far from the
entrance. "Stay here, boy."

Storm nudged his nose into Tom's
shoulder.

"Silver should stay here, too," Tom
said.

He turned around to see that Silver
had already clambered into the first
cart and had sat down, his tongue
lolling, as if he was patiently waiting
for Tom and Elenna to join him.

"Silver, come out of there, right
now!" Elenna said.

The wolf didn't move.

Tom couldn't help grinning. "He's
certainly loyal," he said. "And his

keen nose might be useful down the mine."

Elenna sighed. "All right," she said, climbing into the cart. "But it's going to be a tight squeeze."

Saying goodbye to the miner, who was unloading his tools and supplies, Tom gave the cart a heave to get it rolling. He ran behind it as fast as he could, and jumped in as soon as it picked up speed.

He heard the miner's voice echoing along the tunnel behind them. "Good luck! Take care of each other."

The cart rattled along the railway track, down a twisting, torch-lit passage. At first, thin rays of daylight pierced the darkness through cracks in the roof, but as

they went further into the mine,
the only light came from torches,
reflecting off the damp walls with an
eerie glow.

Tom clung to the side of the cart,
enjoying the swift ride over the dips
and peaks in the tunnel floor.

"Tom," said Elenna, grabbing his
arm. "What if the other miners ask

more questions than the blind man?"

"You're right," Tom said. "We need
to stop before we get to the main
part of the mine."

He wasn't sure how much time
they had left. Already the cart had
carried them deep underground.

As they bumped along the uneven
track, Tom climbed out of the front

as carefully as he could. Elenna steadied him until he planted his feet on the metal tracks, gripping the edges of the cart. The cart slowed down as Tom pressed his feet as hard as he could against the rails.

Sparks sprayed from the wheels as they screeched to a halt.

As the sound died away, Tom could hear faint voices and the noise of hammer blows in the distance. "The other miners," he said. "We'd better keep quiet."

Elenna nodded. She scrambled from the cart and Silver leapt out after her.

Tom led the way cautiously down the tunnel. Soon they passed a place where the track forked; one branch led into deep darkness. Tom and Elenna kept going along the other, torch-lit, tunnel.

The sounds of mining grew gradually louder. Ahead, Tom could see a blood-red light. Soon the tunnel opened up into a vast cavern. A few jagged holes in the roof let in daylight, striking down through the red glow filling the cave. Tom and Elenna pressed themselves to the tunnel wall and peered inside.

"Look!" Elenna breathed.

Dozens of men were hacking at the walls. Their shoulders were slumped, their blows slow and unsteady, as if they were exhausted. Some of them were scooping chunks of rock into sacks; Tom saw something glint in the light. He nudged Elenna.

"They're mining gold!" he whispered.

Other men were carrying the sacks of gold to pile them in more carts at the track's end. Each man kept a hand on the shoulder of the one in front as they moved clumsily across the cavern.

Tom felt his stomach lurch. "They're all blind!" he whispered.

"But how? Why?" Elenna murmured.

As Tom's eyes became used to the red light, he saw that it was emanating from a red jewel embedded in the opposite wall. Above the jewel, he saw two glowing orange eyes.

Instinctively, Tom's hand went to his sword. *Those are the eyes of the bat fiend!*

THE SIGHT-STEALER

Tom squinted through the dim
red light. He made out huge, thick
leathery wings wrapped around the
body of a bat, hanging upside down.

So that is the 'master', Tom
thought. *Fang.*

On the opposite side of the cavern,
one of the slave workers suddenly
dropped his pickaxe, staggered a few
paces away from the cavern wall and

collapsed. Elenna started forward to help him, but Tom grabbed her wrist. "I know it's hard to do nothing," he said. "But we can't give ourselves away."

Elenna nodded reluctantly and gestured to Silver to also stay back. Tom's gaze turned back to the mine. Horror crept through him as he saw that not one of the workers moved to help the fallen miner.

"Get up, Zak," one of them shouted.

"You have to keep working!" another added.

But even while they called out to their fellow slave, they kept swinging their pickaxes at the cavern wall.

"They're too frightened to stop working," Tom muttered. "Just like the man outside."

The fallen worker kept trying to push himself to his feet, but every time he tried, he collapsed again. Tom saw desperation in the miner's eyes.

"We can't just stand here," Elenna whispered, her voice full of anguish.

Before Tom could reply, an ear-piercing screech echoed through the cavern, and a bat-shaped shadow cut through the red haze. A strong gust of air blew Tom's hair back and he pressed himself into the darkness of the tunnel. The vast bat hanging above the jewel had suddenly descended from the cavern roof, wings spread wide and orange eyes glowing with menace; its pointed ears twitched in the gloom.

"Fang…" Elenna whispered.

Teeth bared and claws extended, the bat fiend swooped to grab the fallen worker.

As it got closer, Tom's vision blurred,

as if a grey fog was swirling around him. Then he felt Elenna's hands clutching his arm. "What's happening?" she hissed. "I can't see!"

Tom blinked furiously until his vision cleared. When he gazed out again across the cavern, both the bat and the worker had gone.

Throughout this terrible incident, the other miners hadn't stopped working for a moment. Instead, their pickaxe blows rang out even faster.

Beside Elenna, Silver was standing stiff-legged, his fur bristling, a low growl coming from his throat. Fang may have been a giant bat, but Silver wasn't scared one bit.

"Did your vision blur, as well?" Elenna whispered.

Tom nodded. "The miner outside with the wagon was blind," he said. "And all the workers here are blind, as well. This must be Fang's work. Did you notice that our vision only blurred when he swooped down from the roof?"

"Yes, and now he's gone back again, we can see properly," Elenna agreed.

"Ordinary bats don't have good eyesight," Tom continued. "But Fang *does*. He must be stealing it from the people close to him."

Elenna drew in a sharp breath. "He's the cruellest Beast we've ever faced!"

Tom clenched his fists. "Perhaps," he said. "But to get the jewel that we need for Freya's potion, we must fight him."

"That's not all we must do," Elenna said. "Whatever happens, we can't leave these poor blind men down here."

Silver whined softly, as if he was agreeing with her.

Tom rubbed his eyes, suddenly feeling very tired. A shiver of dread went through him as he remembered his mother's tortured face in his dream. How much time did they have to save her?

But he couldn't deny that Elenna was right. "I know. First we'll free the miners. And *then* Fang had better watch out!"

SLAVERY

"We'll have to pretend to be new workers," said Tom. "That way, we can find out more about this mine."

Elenna nodded and crouched down in front of Silver. "Stay, boy," she said, stroking his head. "We won't be long."

Silver let out another soft whine, but settled down obediently beside the tunnel wall.

Tom led the way across the cavern.

As they neared the opposite wall, one of the miners glanced over his shoulder, though he didn't stop working.

"Who's there?" he called roughly.

"We're the new workers," Tom replied. "I'm Tom. This is Elenna."

"You'll be Toby's replacements, I suppose," he said.

"And about time, too," a second miner added. "My name's Jed. This is Hal."

Tom shared a glance with Elenna; the miner outside had also mentioned Toby. "What happened to Toby?" he asked.

"The master doesn't like people who ask questions," Hal said.

While he was speaking, Jed muttered

something, his words half drowned by the blows of his pickaxe. Tom caught the word 'rebelling'.

"The master also doesn't like workers standing around doing nothing," Hal continued. "Your tools are over there." He gestured to a spot further along the rock face.

Tom and Elenna hurried over and collected pickaxes from a jumbled heap. Then they found places at the rock face between Jed and Hal.

When Tom first swung the pickaxe, the blow jarred his arms. He had struck the rock with all his strength, but he only made a small scratch.

"This is really hard," he whispered to Elenna.

"Aye, hard enough," Jed said. "But

it's good work. You're lucky to be sent here."

Tom spotted Elenna rolling her eyes. She clearly didn't agree!

As he was hacking at the rock face, Tom turned to Jed. "We passed a flooded town on our travels," he said. "Did the water come from here?"

"You must come from a long way away if you don't know that," Jed replied. "The town used to be our home. We thought it was terrible when the flood came, but then an old man came by—" Suddenly, he became aware that he had paused in his working, and broke off to attack the rock face furiously.

Hal took up the story: "The old man said he'd found gold in the old

reservoir. We came to work here.
It made up for losing our homes.
Besides," he added, puffing his
chest out proudly, "all of Kayonia
depends on our gold. It's made us all
very rich!"

Rich? Tom thought, hardly able to

believe what he was hearing. *When you're stuck here, blinded, and working until you collapse?*

"That's right," Jed agreed. Lowering his voice so Tom could scarcely hear the faint murmur beneath the sound of the pickaxes, he added, "There's a rumour that only strong magic could have sensed the gold buried here."

Tom froze in mid-swing, his pickaxe in the air. *Velmal!* Anger coursed through him at the thought of the Evil Wizard ruining these people's lives.

"Magic?" Elenna echoed. Tom could see fury in her eyes. "Aren't you scared to work here?"

"No," Jed replied. "I reckon it was

good magic. Even though we've lost our sight, we're grateful for the work. It means our families up above are well looked after."

"That's right," Hal chimed in. "There's a brand-new town a few leagues north, where they get to stay while we work. We even get to see them every few days."

"It's a small price to pay." Jed gave the rock face an even more forceful whack as if to show how hard he was prepared to work. Hal joined in. Tom knew the time for talk had passed.

Sweat was already trickling down Tom's back, though he had only been working for a short time. Mining the gold was even harder than working in Uncle Henry's forge. He couldn't believe these men had allowed themselves to become slaves. *There have to be easier ways to earn a living!*

When Tom and Elenna had been working for a while, Tom fetched a sack and scooped the rock into it. Fragments of gold glittered within the stone. Elenna helped Tom haul the sack across the mine to a waiting cart. "The Beast hasn't just stolen their sight," Tom whispered. "He's brainwashed them as well!"

Elenna nodded. "We have to find a way of helping them."

But as they returned to the rock face and went on struggling to chip off the gold, Tom couldn't think what to do. There didn't seem to be any way of getting the workers out of the mine without the bat fiend noticing.

Suddenly, a loud screech echoed through the cavern. Tom straightened up, peering into the red shadows under the roof, expecting to spot the Beast swooping down on another doomed miner. But, instead, he saw the miners throwing down their tools.

"That's the signal to stop work," Jed told Tom and Elenna. "Now we go to our sleeping quarters."

While he was speaking, the slaves arranged themselves into a line, each man with his hand on the shoulder of the one in front. Slowly, they began to shuffle across the cave floor towards the carts on the track that would take them out of the mine.

As Tom and Elenna fell in beside them, Tom noticed that he couldn't make out the waiting carts clearly. However much he blinked, they looked fuzzy around the edges.

Horror seized him in an icy grip. *Just being near the Beast is starting to make my sight fade, just like the miners! I have to do something – fast!*

THE TRACK TO FREEDOM

"Is your sight blurred?" Tom whispered to Elenna.

His friend gave him a scared nod. "We have to get out – all of us!"

As he moved slowly across the cavern floor beside the slaves, Tom had an idea. "Remember the way we came in?" he murmured. "We passed a fork in the track. The other direction must lead to the sleeping quarters."

Elenna suddenly looked hopeful. "Do you think we could make the carts change course, and take us outside instead?"

"We can try," said Tom. "But we'll need to be in the first cart."

"I know how we can do that," Elenna said confidently.

She quickened her pace until she reached the front of the line of workers. Tom followed, catching up in time to hear her speaking to the lead miner.

"I've never been to the sleeping quarters before. I'm really scared."

Tom stifled a laugh. If the miners only knew how brave Elenna was!

The miner grunted. "They're just caves, girl. What's to be afraid of?"

"Can I go in the first cart?" she asked. "Just so I know what's happening?"

Tom grew tense as the miner hesitated, but then he gave a curt nod. "Fine."

"I'll go with her," Tom said, putting an arm around Elenna's shoulders. "Well done!" he added to Elenna in a whisper, as she clambered into the first cart. "I'd never have thought of that."

Tom gave the cart a strong push to get it rumbling along the track, and then jumped in himself. As the cart rattled away down slightly sloping tracks, he started as he heard something else land behind him.

"It's only Silver!" Elenna laughed.

Tom glanced back to see the wolf standing behind him, his amber eyes gleaming in the torchlight. The other carts carrying the miners followed them along the track.

"The fork's coming up, I think," Elenna said.

Peering ahead, Tom spotted where the track divided. "There's a lever," he said, pointing to a metal rod that stuck up beside the rails. "If I can move it over, it should change the carts' course."

Tom drew his sword and climbed up onto the edge of the cart. He felt Elenna take two handfuls of his tunic to help him balance steadily.

As the cart swept past, Tom swung his sword at the lever. It flipped over. Just ahead, the rails switched and the whole line of carts rattled along the track that led outside.

"Yes!" Tom yelled triumphantly, easing back into the cart.

At first, the miners didn't realise what had happened, but as the carts drew closer to the mine entrance, Tom heard some confused muttering from the cart behind him.

"What's going on?" one man asked.

"Where's the master taking us now?" another grumbled. "I've done my work. I want food and rest."

"Shh!" a third man warned him. "You'll make the master angry. He—"

A furious shriek sounded from the

tunnel behind. The miners' muttering became yells of terror. Tom felt as though his heart had stopped beating.

"Fang's spotted us!" he hissed.

Turning around, Tom made out the shadowy shape of the bat fiend flying along the tunnel behind the last cart. His glowing orange eyes were fixed on the escaping slaves,

his sharp teeth bared. Tom was just about able to make out the fur bristling across the Beast's muscular body, because his vision had weakened. The bat fiend was now a blur.

"He steals more of our sight by getting closer!" Tom said urgently to Elenna. "We have to defeat this Beast quickly!"

He sprang out of the cart with Elenna and Silver behind him, and stood beside the track while the rest of the carts rattled towards freedom.

Tom gripped his sword, waiting for the bat fiend to reach him. The flapping of the Beast's wings filled the tunnel and dust clouded the air.

Tom's vision blurred even more as

the Beast closed in. But he knew that he must defeat Fang before he could reach the crucial jewel.

The bat fiend loomed over Tom with another fearsome screech. Tom raised his sword and shield against Fang's wings and claws. Retreating down the tunnel, Tom slashed at the Beast, but his blade slid off the thick fur.

Arrows whizzed over Tom's shoulder – Elenna was helping, but most of her shots sailed wide. *She's losing her sight again*, Tom thought. *We both are...*

His watery eyes stung as he backed out of the tunnel into the sunlight. Now he could hardly see a thing. He swiped vainly with his sword, but hit nothing. *I can't see where to aim, and I can't see where Fang's next strike will come from!*

Then Tom heard another shriek from Fang, but this time the Beast's cry was full of pain and frustration. Squinting, Tom saw Fang hovering in a shaft of sunlight, just inside the tunnel. Smoke was rising from a smouldering spot on his wing. Fang spun around in pain and confusion, as though he didn't know how to escape the light.

"He can't stand the sun!" Tom shouted to Elenna.

Fang retreated into the tunnel, his injured wing drooping as he flapped along clumsily. Within moments he was gone.

"My eyes are starting to clear!" Elenna said with relief.

"Mine, too," Tom responded.

Close by, the miners were clambering out of the carts, still sounding bewildered to be out in the open. Tom knew that he didn't have time to talk to them now. He had a Quest to complete.

"We have to go back in," he said to Elenna, who followed as he led the way towards an empty cart at the end of the tracks. As Elenna climbed in, Silver tried to follow. "No, boy," she said, gently pushing him away. "You must guard the miners."

Silver gave a whine of protest, but sat down obediently, thumping his tail on the ground.

Tom pushed the cart off and then jumped in beside his friend.

They left the sunlight behind as the cart rattled down the tunnel...back towards the Beast.

BLIND COMBAT

As the cart sped along, Tom noticed that the light from the torches looked blurred. *I'm losing my sight again*, he thought. *And I know what that means...*

The bat fiend is close.

A gust of wind ruffled Tom's hair, and he got his shield up just as Fang dropped down from the tunnel roof, battering him around the head and shoulders with his leathery wings. Claws scraped across his shield, trying to tear it from his grasp, and Tom fell back against the side of the cart, jarring every bone in his body.

Tom swung his sword, but the blow missed as the cart carried them away from the Beast. Fang let out a screech of rage and frustration. With a powerful flap of his uninjured wing, he caught up with the cart and clamped his claws down on the edge. Tom let out a cry of alarm as the cart tipped over.

Tom and Elenna were flung out of the cart. Hitting the ground hard, Tom groped in the murky light of the torches until he found Elenna's arm and gripped it.

"Are you all right?" he gasped.

"I think so," Elenna replied.

Tom turned to look for Fang. He could just make out the bat fiend on the other side of the upturned cart, flinging it aside. Fang's eyes flashed with pure hatred.

"Elenna," Tom said, "if we're going to go blind fighting this Beast, we'd better stick together. Let's use your rope to tie ourselves to each other, so we always know the other is safe."

"Good idea," Elenna replied. She pulled a length of rope from her quiver and tied one end around her wrist and the other around Tom's.

Blinking, Tom realised that he couldn't see his friend. The torches on the wall were just smudges of light, too dim to show him anything in the tunnel. His sight was now almost completely gone.

I'm fighting blind! he thought, pushing away his fear. *Then so be it. I'll fight on, whatever happens!*

Tom scrambled to his feet, bumping into Elenna. A flapping sound and another rush of air against his face told him that Fang was nearby. Before he could raise his sword, he felt the slap of the Beast's wing against his shoulder, so hard that it almost drove him to his knees.

Somehow, Tom managed to stay on his feet. He slashed out, feeling his sword rake across a leathery wing, and hearing the Beast let out a ferocious screech that made Tom's head hurt. He took a step back, feeling a tug from the rope that bound him to Elenna.

"Keep your back to the wall!" he said with a gasp. "That way, Fang can't attack us from behind."

Gripping his sword hilt with both hands, he thrust the blade forward, but found only empty air. The flap of wings above his head alerted him; he swung his sword up just in time to ward off Fang as the bat fiend dropped on him from above.

My hearing is getting sharper! Tom realised. Though all he could see of Fang was a shadowy outline in the darkness, he could *hear* the Beast perfectly – every hiss of fury and swish of his wings through the air.

Tom lashed out in the direction of the sound and heard a snarl as Fang dodged his attack.

"Not so easy now, is it?" Tom taunted Fang. "You've taken my sight, but I can still hear you!"

At the same moment, he heard a cry of triumph from Elenna. "I can

hear him! I know exactly where to shoot!"

Tom froze, listening to the scraping of claws on stone. The Beast was trying to sneak up on him by inching along the tunnel floor! He swung his sword downwards and felt it strike Fang's body.

The bat fiend shrieked in pain and launched into the air. Tom felt warm blood dripping onto his arm.

I've wounded him! Tom thought, beginning to believe that he could win this battle.

For the moment, the Beast had drawn back; Tom's ears picked up his angry growls. His hearing was now so sharp that he could even make out Fang's heartbeat. He stepped forward hesitantly, homing in on the sounds.

Fang rushed through the air again, so quickly that he knocked Tom back against the wall with his good wing. Tom stumbled and fell, his sword clattering from his hand. The Beast screeched in triumph.

Frantically, Tom reached for his

sword in the dirt of the tunnel floor. As his fingers closed around the hilt, he heard a new sound amid the screeching. It took a moment for Tom to realise what it was.

"Water!" he exclaimed. Tom groped for the tunnel wall, pressing his ear up against it. "There's water behind the rock face."

"It must be the lake," Elenna said.

Tom pictured the flooded town, and the vast expanse of water that lay just beyond the wall.

That water could drown the bat fiend, he thought. *Or force him out into the sunlight. There's only one problem – how do I get it to flood the caves?*

9

FLOOD!

Before Tom could work out how
to free the dammed water, Fang
attacked again. Tom brought up his
shield and scrambled backwards,
dragging Elenna with him by the
rope that bound them together.
He spotted a ray of sunlight shining
down from a chink in the tunnel
roof, momentarily lighting up his
murky view.

"This way!" he urged Elenna. "Fang won't dare fly through the light."

"That won't defeat him, though," Elenna pointed out.

"I know," said Tom, sheathing his sword. "But I have an idea!"

He fumbled in the bag tied to his waist, searching for the magic mirror he had collected in Gwildor when he defeated Trema the Earth Lord. When it caught sunlight, the mirror could make holes in even the hardest surfaces. He could hear Fang snarling as he tried to get past the ray of light.

"Hurry!" Elenna said. "The light won't hold Fang back for ever."

Tom pulled out the magic mirror.

Hazy twinkles of light shone from where the diamonds on its back glittered in the sunlight. Tom almost wished that he could see it properly.

Tom angled the mirror in the shaft of light so that the light reflected off the mirror and hit the tunnel wall. Soon, Tom smelt smoke and heard debris trickling down the wall, followed by a fierce hissing sound. Finally, he felt a thin jet of water spraying his face. He had made a hole in the wall!

"It's working!" Elenna exclaimed.

A loud cracking sound almost drowned out her words. Then *WHOOSH!* Water gushed out.

"Here it comes!" Tom yelled. He staggered as it blasted into him and swept him and Elenna off their feet.

Tom felt the cords that fastened the bag of Gwildorian tokens to his belt loosen in the force of the water. He grabbed for it, but all he felt was cold, rushing water. The current had stolen the bag!

No! Tom thought, remembering all his struggles to win the tokens. *I'll never find them again!* He struggled to stay afloat as the flood carried him and his friend further down into the mine. He felt the rope joining them stretching tight, pulling against his wrist. Then, as the water rolled him over again, the rope started to coil around his chest.

Tom couldn't see Fang, but he could hear him shrieking and

thrashing. One of his claws slapped him, knocking Tom dizzy.

Tom sank beneath the surface.

Underwater, Tom shook his head clear and swam upwards. He took in a grateful breath of air, seeing a blur of pure light overhead. He realised that they had been carried back into the huge cavern where the miners had been working. Sunlight danced on the surface of the flood from gaps and crevices in the roof that drew slowly closer as the water rose.

Tom heard Fang's wings lashing at the water. The Beast was screeching in agony as the sunlight hit him.

Tom's sight was beginning to clear. He could actually make out the shape of the drowning bat fiend

as he was forced into a patch of sunlight from one of the biggest gaps in the roof. The Beast struggled more fiercely, wings thrashing and clawed feet kicking. Its shrieks shook the walls for a moment longer, before fading away to gargled, choking noises. Then, its body exploded into hundreds of tiny bats that fluttered away harmlessly into the open air.

"You've done it, Tom!" Elenna spluttered. "We've won!"

Relief flooded through Tom as he watched the end of the Evil Beast.

"It's not over yet," he panted, tilting his head back to keep his mouth and nose above the surface. "If we can't escape from the water, we'll drown."

It was hard for Tom and Elenna to swim because the rope that tied them together kept dragging them under the water. Tom felt as if his chest was going to burst as he fought his way to the surface so he could breathe. If only he still had the bag of Gwildorian tokens; in the bag was a pearl that allowed him to breathe underwater.

"Here, take this," he shouted, handing his shield to Elenna. "It should keep you afloat. I need to draw my sword."

When his hand was free, Tom pulled his sword from its sheath and sawed through the rope that bound him to Elenna. Now they could swim properly.

Tom gasped for breath as he looked for a way out. The rising floodwater was carrying them towards the gaps in the cavern roof.

"We'll be able to climb out soon," he said.

Suddenly, Tom remembered why he had come into the caves. "The red jewel!" he exclaimed. "I must go back for it, or my mother will die!"

Tom ducked his head under the water and looked for it. He could just make out the shining jewel. Tom resurfaced, shaking his eyes clear of water. Then he took a huge breath and plunged below the surface, striking out towards the hazy red glow.

By the time Tom reached the place

where the jewel was embedded in the cavern wall, his lungs were on fire and his arms were drained of strength.

The weight of the water made everything seem heavier as Tom struggled to prise the jewel out of the wall with the tip of his sword. *It's no good*, he thought. *I'm going to have to go back for air. Wait...* The jewel started to come loose from the wall. It was coming free! Tom grabbed it before it sank out of sight.

Now, swim! he told himself.

As he broke the surface, Tom sucked in lungfuls of air. Elenna was treading water beside him.

"You found it!" she cried, pointing

at the glowing jewel in Tom's hand.

"Yes!" Tom gasped. "And now
we—"

He broke off as his head brushed
the underside of the cavern roof.

"The water's still rising!" he cried.
"We have to get out of here!"

10

A MIXED BLESSING

Tom could see light coming from an opening in the roof near the other side of the cavern. With Elenna just behind him, he swam towards it. When he reached the pool of light he stretched up through the hole and dragged himself out, his wet clothes weighing heavily on him as he slumped down on the muddy ground.

Elenna was still treading water.

She handed Tom's shield up to him, then he reached down to help her scramble out of the flooded mine.

"We made it!" he said, collapsing on his back.

As he stared up at the sky, Tom saw the clouds gradually come into sharp focus.

"My sight has come back," he exclaimed. "Just as good as it always was!"

Beside him he heard Elenna laugh with delight. "Mine, too!" she replied. "I was frightened Fang had stolen it for ever."

"Fang won't steal anyone's sight ever again," Tom said with satisfaction.

He stood up and looked around. He

and Elenna had emerged at the top of a gentle slope overlooking the pit. The freed miners were still huddled near the end of the tracks. Tom spotted Storm waiting under the tree, with Silver beside him. Floodwater had gushed out of the tunnel, turning the bottom of the pit to a muddy lake, but already its force had died away to a trickle.

"Come on," Tom said to Elenna. "We should talk to the workers."

His feet squelching in his boots, Tom led the way down to the pit. Storm let out a welcoming whinny and Silver bounded over to Elenna, jumping up and waving his tail.

Tom approached the group of miners. "You're free!" he announced, wondering why they were still standing around. "You can go home."

One of the miners turned to him; Tom recognised Jed. He squinted at Tom, blinking watery eyes. His sight must be coming back, too.

"We haven't got homes," he said.

"We lived in the mine, and now it's flooded... Thanks to you."

"Yes," Hal added, coming up to stand beside Jed. "We'll be poor now. We might even starve!"

Tom exchanged a shocked glance with Elenna. *I thought they'd be happy to be free!*

Then he reminded himself that Velmal had poisoned the workers' minds: he had convinced them that they needed the gold. When the evil magic wore off, surely the men would realise that losing the mine was a small price to pay for being able to see?

"You'll soon be able to see clearly again," Tom assured them. "Then you can find other jobs, anywhere in the kingdom."

"We don't want jobs anywhere else," Jed shouted, his face reddening. "The mine kept us close to our ruined town. We don't want to be scattered all over Kayonia."

Tom understood that. Even though he willingly travelled on his Beast Quests, he missed his family back in Avantia. Families and friends would want to stay together.

"Your town isn't flooded any more," Elenna pointed out. "Once the water's completely gone, you can go back there."

The miners looked at each other, muttering together and shaking their heads. They obviously weren't convinced.

"Life was even harder before the

town was flooded," Hal grumbled.

Eventually the miners moved off in a straggling line, heading for a path that would take them to the top of the pit and back towards their old town. Several of them cast regretful glances back at the tunnel as they went, their eyes narrowed in anger.

Watching them, Tom felt a shudder of doubt. "What if Velmal's magic never wears off?" he said.

Elenna nodded, with a worried frown. "The men have spent a long time underground. They might not be able to live an ordinary life any more."

"And they said the whole kingdom relies on the gold from the mine," Tom added. "Could we have just done

Kayonia more harm than good?"

Silver pressed himself to Elenna's side, while Storm trotted over to nuzzle Tom's shoulder, as if understanding that their masters were troubled.

Sighing, Elenna stroked Silver's head. "We've defeated the Beast, and found the red jewel," she said firmly. "We've done good here, Tom."

Tom met her gaze, about to ask her if she was sure, when a voice sounded from behind him, making them both jump.

"She's right, Tom. You have done the right thing."

Tom spun around to see Marc, Wizard Aduro's apprentice, who was in Kayonia to aid the warrior queen,

Romaine, in her time of trouble.

"Marc!" Tom exclaimed. "I'm so glad to see you!"

Marc smiled as he reached out to take the red jewel from Tom. In exchange, he held out a bag to Tom. It was dripping water, but Tom still recognised it. He could hardly believe what he was seeing.

"My Gwildorian tokens! How did you find them?"

"The flood washed them out of the mine," Marc explained, as Tom gratefully took the bag and fastened it onto his belt again.

"Thank you, Marc," Tom said. "I thought I'd lost them for ever."

"Don't forget that your Quest is only half complete," Marc continued.

"I know," Tom replied. Resolve welled up inside him. Three Beasts defeated. Three more Beasts to go. He squared his shoulders and looked at the land of Kayonia spilling out before him. "While there's blood in my veins," he said, "I will always prevail!"

CONGRATULATIONS, YOU HAVE COMPLETED THIS QUEST!

At the end of each chapter you were awarded a special gold coin.
The QUEST in this book was worth an amazing 11 coins.

Look at the Beast Quest totem picture inside the back cover of this book to see how far you've come in your journey to become

MASTER OF THE BEASTS.

The more books you read, the more coins you will collect!

Do you want your own
Beast Quest Totem?

1. Cut out and collect the coin below
2. Go to the Beast Quest website
3. Download and print out your totem
4. Add your coin to the totem
www.beastquest.co.uk/totem

11

Don't miss the next exciting Beast Quest book, MURK THE SWAMP MAN!

Read on for a sneak peek...

CHAPTER ONE

GOLD RUSH

"Tom, back there in the gold mine, I wasn't sure we were going to defeat Fang," Elenna confessed, as she edged around a bend on the steep mountain pass. Silver, her wolf, raced ahead of her, clearly pleased to be leaving the dark tunnels of the mine behind. "Velmal's magic made him so powerful."

Tom gently pulled on Storm's reins and led the stallion along a tricky part of the rocky trail. Memories of his battle with the mighty bat fiend filled his mind: the massive leathery wings, his sharp fangs and claws. "The Beasts of Kayonia are the strongest we've ever faced," he admitted. "But we can't stop, not when my mother—"

Tom broke off, swallowing hard. Just thinking of how Freya was entrapped by Velmal almost suffocated him with rage. He knew she was nearing death with every passing day. If he didn't defeat the Evil Wizard, she wouldn't survive.

He gazed out across Kayonia, grateful that his eyesight had returned to normal. One of Fang's evil powers had been to steal people's sight. From their position on the mountainside, Tom could see the whole land spread out below him.

It was not as beautiful as Gwildor or Avantia, but Tom was sure that Kayonia had once been a great kingdom. Queen Romaine could make it so again. He took a deep, calming breath, remembering the magical ingredients from the six Beasts of Kayonia. These ingredients could make the potion that would save Freya and destroy Velmal's magic.

"Don't worry, we already have three of the ingredients," Elenna said softly. "The Black Cactus, the jade ring and the red jewel."

Tom glanced at his friend in amazement. "How did you know what I was thinking?" he asked.

Elenna shrugged. "Remember how many Quests we've been on. Of course I know what you're thinking!" She gazed at him. "I came with you to Kayonia so that we could save your mother, and that's what we're going to do."

Tom smiled at his brave friend, recalling their adventures so far. With Elenna, Storm and Silver by his side, Tom felt like he could do anything. Although he might be far from his home in Avantia, at least he had his friends with him on this journey.

He reached for the amulet that hung from his neck and rested it in his palm. He turned it over to see the map of Kayonia – a map so real that Tom could see the rivers flowing past the mountains, and valleys etched across the silver disc. He felt a rush of excitement as he saw a fresh path magically appear on the map. The trail sped across the surface of the amulet towards an immense swamp in the north-west. The word *MURK* appeared next to it in swirly writing.

"Where's the Beast's image?" Elenna asked.

Tom shrugged. During all of their Quests in Kayonia, the amulet had always shown them the form of Velmal's Beasts. "He must be hiding somewhere. We'll discover what Murk looks like when we reach the swamp. While there's blood in my veins, I will find and defeat this Beast."

They continued to make their way down the mountain, each taking turns to lead Storm. Silver ran out in front. Tom was relieved that the mountain trail was easier to descend than it had been to climb, and as the sun rose higher in the sky, he and Elenna jumped into Storm's saddle and cantered onwards.

As they finally stepped onto Kayonia's flat plains and travelled along a deserted road, Tom felt

Elenna's exhausted body sag against his. He gently nudged her in the ribs and she gave a yelp of surprise, sitting bolt upright in the saddle.

"Sorry about that." Tom turned in the saddle, with a grin. "But I can't have you falling asleep or you might slip off!"

Elenna yawned and stretched her arms. "My body has no idea what time it is. Nightfall in this kingdom is so sudden, I never know when to sleep."

"I can't get used to it either," Tom admitted, as they rounded a bend in the road. "I wonder how Kayonian people manage it."

"We'll be able to ask them ourselves." Elenna pointed

ahead over his shoulder. "There's a village over there. We can stop for some food."

"And a rest," Tom added. "We'll both need it before we face Murk in the swamp."

Read
MURK THE SWAMP MAN
to find out more!

FIGHT THE BEASTS,
FEAR THE MAGIC

Are you a BEAST QUEST mega fan?
Do you want to know about all the latest news,
competitions and books before anyone else?

Then join our Quest Club!

Visit the BEAST QUEST website
and sign up today!

www.beastquest.co.uk

Discover the new Beast Quest mobile game from

Available free on iOS and Android

Guide Tom on his Quest to free the Good Beasts
of Avantia from Malvel's evil spells.

Battle the Beasts, defeat the minions,
unearth the secrets and collect
rewards as you journey through the
Kingdom of Avantia.

DOWNLOAD THE APP TO BEGIN
THE ADVENTURE NOW!

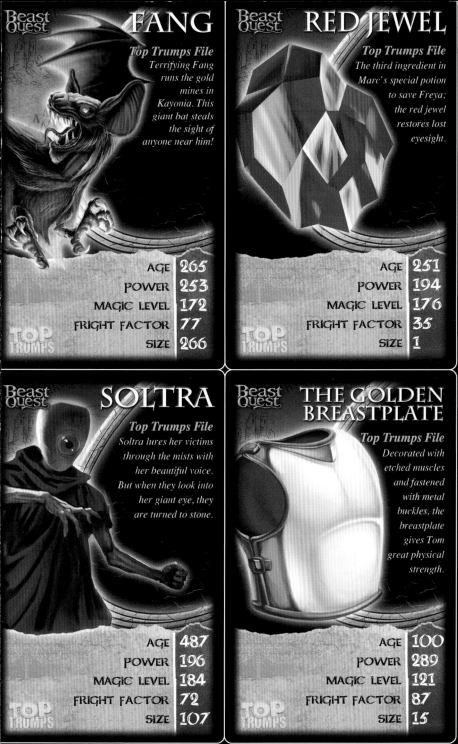

FANG

Top Trumps File
Terrifying Fang runs the gold mines in Kayonia. This giant bat steals the sight of anyone near him!

AGE	265
POWER	253
MAGIC LEVEL	172
FRIGHT FACTOR	77
SIZE	266

RED JEWEL

Top Trumps File
The third ingredient in Marc's special potion to save Freya; the red jewel restores lost eyesight.

AGE	251
POWER	194
MAGIC LEVEL	176
FRIGHT FACTOR	35
SIZE	1

SOLTRA

Top Trumps File
Soltra lures her victims through the mists with her beautiful voice. But when they look into her giant eye, they are turned to stone.

AGE	487
POWER	196
MAGIC LEVEL	184
FRIGHT FACTOR	72
SIZE	107

THE GOLDEN BREASTPLATE

Top Trumps File
Decorated with etched muscles and fastened with metal buckles, the breastplate gives Tom great physical strength.

AGE	100
POWER	289
MAGIC LEVEL	121
FRIGHT FACTOR	87
SIZE	15